THE PATH

Crisis of Faith

THE PATH

Crisis of Faith

Ron **MARZ**
W R I T E R

Bart **SEARS**
P E N C I L E R

Mark **PENNINGTON**
I N K E R

Michael **ATIYEH**
C O L O R I S T

CHAPTER 5
Walter **SIMONSON** · ILLUSTRATOR

Dave **LANPHEAR** · LETTERER

CrossGeneration Comics   **Oldsmar, Florida**

Crisis of Faith

features Prequel
and Chapters 1-6
of the ongoing series
THE PATH

THE PATH • PREQUEL

I am the warlord Todosi.

I am of the clan Tsugawa. My father was a daimyo of the Kojima province in the north, and our great house has served the Emperor for two hundred years.

The Tsugawas were instrumental in keeping the Ohira Dynasty upon the throne during the Wada Rebellion. But that conflict claimed my father's life and saw the destruction of our ancestral estate.

While my brother pursued enlightenment, I dedicated myself to the military and rose quickly through the ranks. Yes, my skill with the dotanuki distinguished me, but it was the Ohiras' indebtedness to my family that assured my career.

I became warlord of Nayado's armies, and answered directly to the Emperor Mitsumune himself. The forces of my nation are his sword to wield, but I am the hand that holds the blade.

*M*y comrades in this
are not what is
expected, but they have
spilled blood for me and
I have bled with them.

*A*lways to my left is Wulf, an outlander hailing
from lands far distant from ours. He is as a mountain,
a warrior whose sheer ferocity I have yet to see matched.

*T*o my right is Yamane Aiko,
delicate and deadly. I am not
fond of the notion of female samurai,
but Aiko is any man's equal. She has
come to mean more to me than simply
a strong sword to match my own.

I would have no
others at my side.

Our lives belong to the Emperor Mitsumune, who sits upon the Throne of Petals in his castle at Yazaki.

Mitsumune has been my friend since childhood. We played together as boys. We shared adventures as young men. I love him as I love my own brother.

Of late, though, I begin to wonder if his duties do not tax him too greatly. There are times when he is not the man I know, certainly not the boy whose nose I bloodied as we pretended to be sumo.

Where Mitsumune's ascension reere once past, here he is ... Imperial Babe. The whispers at court had already begun when he called me before him and commanded the unthinkable.

Mitsumune bade me attack the empire of Shinacea, which crouches across the Tsuneo Channel on our western shores like an insatiable beast poised to devour lesser prey.

Nayado is a mouse to the great dragon of Shinacea. We are outnumbered a hundred to one. But my Emperor has said that it must be so, and I have no choice but to obey.

I gathered my troops and told them to prepare to conquer the bloated enemy to the west.

I told them they were the finest warriors of any land. I told them their bravery was without peer.

I did not tell them we had no hope of victory.

We attempted a landing upon Shinacea's shores, but found its vast army awaiting us. My warriors were indeed the finest and bravest of any land.

And still they were slaughtered.

*M*ore than half my army perished there, so many that the sea turned to blood. Our losses would have been even greater had I not called the retreat when I did.

*S*o dragging our wounded with us we fled back across the sea, and I prepared to go before my Emperor and pay the price failure demands.

But it seems I will not have that chance. Shinacea's anger was piqued by our arrogance. Their army has followed us across the sea, and now fouls Nayado's soil beneath its boot heels.

The remnants of my soldiers prepare to make a final stand here, on ground that has absorbed the blood of so many battles. These plains are the gateway to Yazaki, and each life that defends it will be dearly sold.

This night I prayed. I lifted pleas to the same gods whom my brother has embraced. I prayed for delivery, so that Nayado might not be wiped from the face of the earth.

And my prayers were answered. A woman unknown to me appeared, a woman possessed of fiery eyes, who set upon my flesh a mark of the gods, a symbol of their favor.

Now, as I wait for the sun to crest the horizon, I am ready to perform my last duty for my Emperor. There is power in this sigil with which I have been graced.

But I do not know if it is the mark of our salvation...

YES, I'M SURE YOU ARE.

WE WANT YOU TO BE A *FAT* LITTLE MOUSE.

MY LORD?

THE DIARY?

YOU DIDN'T SAY HELLO TO MY FRIEND, YUKIO. HE'S A *PLUMP* LITTLE ONE, ISN'T HE?

WHAT A *LUCKY* MOUSE YOU ARE. NO ONE IS ALLOWED WITHIN THESE WALLS SAVE THE EMPEROR HIMSELF.

ARE THESE NOT THE MOST *EXQUISITE* GARDENS IN ALL SHINACEA?

IN ALL THE *WORLD*?

SOMETIMES THE VERY SMALL HAVE *GOOD REASON* TO FEAR THE VERY LARGE.

I HAVE *NEVER* BEEN VERY SMALL.

SO. TELL ME OF THE COURT OF THE WISE AND KIND EMPEROR MITSUMUNE OF NAYADO.

IS HIS *TONGUE* STILL LOOSE AROUND HIS CONCUBINES?

NAYADO STILL REELS FROM THE DEFEAT OF ITS ARMY.

MY GENERALS *ALSO* TELL ME TALES OF *GODS* DESCENDING FROM THE HEAVENS TO THE BATTLEFIELD.

THEY TELL ME TODOSI WAS *SLAIN* BY ONE OF THESE GODS.

COME, *COME,* MY LITTLE FRIEND.

ALL TRUE?

ALL TRUE, MY LORD, THOUGH EVEN *I* AM NOT CERTAIN WHAT IT ALL MEANS.

EVENTS TOOK A MOST *UNEXPECTED* TURN.

DID THEY? AND HOW COULD *YOU* KNOW OF THINGS THAT OCCUR BEYOND YAZAKI'S WALLS?

MY GENERALS TELL ME VICTORY WAS *OURS.*

SHINACEA'S MIGHT *OVERWHELMED* NAYADO'S DEFENDERS.

AND YET OUR ARMIES FLED BACK ACROSS THE SEA BEFORE WE COULD PRESS A FINAL TRIUMPH.

BEFORE I HELD NAYADO IN MY HANDS.

DON'T BE AFRAID. IT'S ALL RIGHT.

THERE'S A GOOD BOY.

THERE'S A *BRAVE* BOY.

I HAVE MY WAYS, DO I NOT?

DAWN BROUGHT THE BATTLE...

...EVEN BEFORE
THE MORNING
FOG HAD LIFTED.

I SAW
IT ALL.

THE MARK
TODOSI
BORE MADE HIM
THE EQUAL OF
TEN MEN. OF A
HUNDRED MEN.

HE FOUGHT AS
THOUGH HE
WAS DEATH ITSELF
GIVEN FORM.

HIS SWORD LEFT
A WAKE OF
CARNAGE EVERY-
WHERE IT STRUCK.

*S*TIRRED BY THEIR
WARLORD'S
EXAMPLE, NAYADO'S
SONS STRUGGLED
FIERCELY, NOT FOR
THEIR OWN SURVIVAL,
BUT FOR THAT OF
THEIR ENTIRE NATION.

*I*T WAS
GLORIOUS...

...BUT NOT
NEARLY
ENOUGH.

SHINACEA'S
STRENGTH OF
NUMBERS WAS
IRRESISTABLE.
EACH SOLDIER
WHO PERISHED
WAS REPLACED
BY TWO MORE.

TOPOSI
REALIZED THE
HOPELESSNESS
OF THE BATTLE
AND FELL TO HIS
KNEES IN DESPAIR.
HE CRIED OUT TO
THE GODS...

...AND THIS
TIME THEY
APPEARED
TO HIM.

HERE YOUR
OWN FORCES
BROKE RANKS AND
RAN, LORD, FEARING
AN OPPONENT WHO
COULD CALL DOWN
THE GODS FROM
THEIR HEAVEN.

SUCH WAS
THE LOYALTY
OF TOPOSI'S
MEN THAT,
THINKING THEIR
WARLORD WAS
THREATENED,
THEY SURGED
FORWARD AND
ATTACKED THE
GODS.

THE GODS
SHOWED
THEM NO MERCY.

SEETHING AT SEEING HIS MEN SLAIN LIKE DOGS, TOPOSI CONFRONTED ONE OF THE GODS AND SPLIT HIM FROM SHOULDER TO GROIN.

BUT THE GOD WAS UNHARMED. MORE, HE WAS ANGERED.

THE GOD TURNED HIS OWN WEAPON UPON TOPOSI, A ROD OF POWER SMALL ENOUGH TO BE HELD IN ONE HAND.

BRIGHT FIRE DESTROYED NAYADO'S WAR-LORD IN THE BLINK OF AN EYE.

BUT IN DYING, TOPOSI SOME-HOW CONSUMED THE GOD AS WELL, REDUCING HIM TO A HUSK.

THE MONK TOBO-SAN CAME TO HIS FALLEN BROTHER'S SIDE AND CLUTCHED HIS BODY AS THE GODS GATHERED AROUND. OBO-SAN CRIED OUT HIS RAGE.

AND THEN, BEFORE THE GODS COULD RETRIEVE IT, HE TOOK UP THE WEAPON OF HEAVEN. THEY FELL BACK IN FEAR OF HIM.

BRANDISHING THEIR OWN WEAPON AGAINST THEM, THE MONK DENOUNCED THEM AS FALSE GODS AND VOWED TO HAVE HIS VENGEANCE UPON THEM.

THE GODS FLED.

WHEN THE MONK ROSE, HE CARRIED NOT ONLY THE WEAPON OF THE GODS IN HIS HAND...

...BUT ALSO THEIR MARK UPON HIS FLESH, INHERITED FROM HIS BROTHER.

I SAW NOTHING MORE...

...BECAUSE I CAME HERE. TO *YOU*.

THIS WEAPON OF HEAVEN. IS IT *KNOWN* TO YOU?

I HAVE NEVER SEEN ITS LIKE.

BUT IT REMAINS IN THE POSSESSION OF TOPOSI'S BROTHER.

THE MONK.

YES...

...THOUGH HE IS A CREATURE OF DUTY. IT SEEMS LIKELY HE WILL PLACE THE WEAPON IN MITSUMUNE'S HANDS.

IF THIS WEAPON IS TRULY AS YOU SAY...

HOW *VERY* FORTUNATE.

BAD BUSINESS, MAKING BARGAINS WITH DEMONS.

THEY'RE DANGEROUS AND UNTRUSTWORTHY, LITTLE ONE, EVEN WHEN THEY'RE BEHOLDEN TO YOU.

BUT SUCH BARGAINS ARE A *NECESSARY EVIL* IN ORDER TO MAINTAIN POWER IN AN EMPIRE AS VAST AS SHINACEA.

DESPITE ITS SIZE SHINACEA HAS *MANY* ENEMIES, MANY LESSER FOES WHO ARE JEALOUS OF OUR GRANDEUR AND WOULD SEE IT DESTROYED.

IT HAS *ALWAYS* BEEN SO...

...WE DEVOUR THEM.

...BUT SHINACEA'S MYRIAD ENEMIES HAVE NEVER SUCCEEDED IN *PULLING DOWN* THE EMPIRE.

IT FALLS TO *ME* TO BE VIGILANT. *I* MUST KEEP SHINACEA SAFE FROM ALL THOSE WHO WOULD ATTACK IT.

SO WE ARE PATIENT. WE WATCH OUR FOES CAREFULLY...

...AND WHEN WE SEE OUR OPPORTUNITY...

NAYADO WILL BE NO DIFFERENT.

WHAT WILL HE DO NOW?

WHAT WILL HE DO?

OBO-SAN.

LOOK AT HIM, AIKO.

HE STILL PERFORMS THE RITUALS TO PREPARE TODOSI'S BODY.

A HOLY MAN WHO WATCHED THE GODS SLAY HIS BROTHER.

A HOLY MAN WHO WATCHED HIS BROTHER SLAY ONE OF THOSE GODS.

AND THEN OBO-SAN SWORE HE WOULD HUNT THEM DOWN AND DESTROY THEM.

AND YET...

...THIS.

PERHAPS HE PERFORMS THE RITUALS TO TEMPER HIS OWN GRIEF.

OR PERHAPS BECAUSE HE IS LOST AND KNOWS NO OTHER WAY.

NO?

THEN WHY *DID* YOU COME HERE, TSUGAWA TODOSI?

NOGAWA CUR.

IF IT'S *STEEL* HE WANTS—

RYUICHI...

...*LET* TODOSI.

YOU INSULT *ME?!*

THE TSUGAWAS HAVE *ALWAYS* BEEN LAP DOGS TO THE OHIRAS...

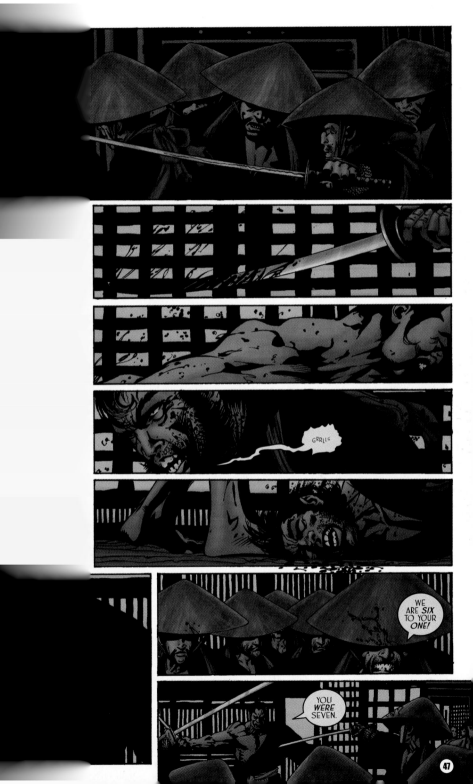

WE ARE *SIX* TO YOUR *ONE!*

YOU *WERE* SEVEN.

47

IT SEEMS SO *NEAR*, DOESN'T IT, RYUICHI?

LIKE YESTERDAY.

AND YET IT WAS SO LONG AGO...

...BUT THIS IS AS MITSUMUNE HAS COMMANDED, AND IT WILL BE SO.

JUST AS HE COMMANDED WE ATTACK SHINACEA AND PROVOKE THE SLEEPING DRAGON?

THE CAMPAIGN WAS *DOOMED* BEFORE IT BEGAN.

BUT TODOSI'S BRAVERY DROVE THE SHINACEAN BARBARIANS FROM OUR SHORES, OBO-SAN.

MIND YOUR *TONGUE*, OBO-SAN. EVEN AROUND THE SERVANTS.

ESPECIALLY AROUND THE SERVANTS.

YES, WE ALL GREW UP TOGETHER, BUT MITSUMUNE IS *EMPEROR* NOW.

IT IS TREASON TO SAY SUCH THINGS. TO EVEN *THINK* THEM.

...AND SO MUCH HAS *CHANGED.*

...AND WE PREPARE FOR MY BROTHER'S *FUNERAL.*

MITSUMUNE SITS UPON THE THRONE OF PETALS, YOU NOW SERVE HIM AS GENERAL OF HIS ARMIES...

UNUSUAL, DON'T YOU THINK, TO HOLD SUCH A CEREMONY WITHIN THE WALLS OF THE ROYAL CASTLE?

MANY THINGS ARE UNUSUAL THESE DAYS, OBO-SAN...

LEAVE US, BOTH OF YOU.

YOUR BROTHER *SAVED* NAYADO.

YES, MY LORD.

IT WOULD NOT HAVE BEEN *NECESSARY* FOR MY BROTHER TO SAVE NAYADO HAD THE EMPEROR NOT PLACED IT IN DANGER.

I COME TO DOUBT IF MITSUMUNE IS FIT TO *RULE.*

NOT SAYING A THING DOES NOT MAKE IT GO AWAY.

TELL ME YOU HAVE NOT HAD THESE THOUGHTS, RYUICHI. MY BROTHER'S DEATH MAKES *YOU* WARLORD.

NOW *YOU* SERVE MITSUMUNE'S WHIMS.

IT BECOMES MORE AND MORE OBVIOUS HIS SENSES ARE AFFLICTED. THE MAD CAMPAIGN AGAINST SHINACEA IS ONLY THE MOST *RECENT* INCIDENT.

MITSUMUNE WILL LEAD NAYADO TO ITS *RUIN.*

THIS IS NOT A DISCUSSION I WILL HAVE WITH YOU. NOT *TODAY,* NOT ANY *OTHER* DAY.

I WILL FORGET THESE WORDS PASSED YOUR LIPS, OBO-SAN. *YOU* WOULD BE WISE TO DO THE SAME.

IT'S SAID THE GODS FAVORED YOUR BROTHER UPON THE BATTLEFIELD.

THE GODS *DESTROYED* MY BROTHER UPON THE BATTLEFIELD.

TOPOSI ALWAYS SERVED THE GODS FAITHFULLY.

HIS REWARD FOR THAT LOYALTY WAS *DEATH*.

I DO.

WHAT DO YOU INTEND TO *DO* WITH IT?

I KNOW NOT THE WEAPON'S *TRUE POWER*...

...BUT I HAVE SWORN MY *VENGEANCE* UPON THE FALSE GODS TO WHOM I ONCE PRAYED.

NO.

THE WEAPON IS *EVIL*. I PONDERED DESTROYING IT BECAUSE IT *IS* A THING OF THE GODS, BUT DID NOT ALLOW MYSELF TO DO SO.

IT IS TOO VALUABLE AS A TOOL FOR MY VENGEANCE.

I WILL LET IT BE USED FOR NO *OTHER* PURPOSE.

THEY'RE HERE.

ENTER.

YOU AND WULF WERE MY BROTHER'S STAUNCHEST COMRADES. I KNOW THIS CANNOT BE AN EASY DAY.

FOR *YOU* ESPECIALLY.

YOUR FAMILY TOOK ME IN WHEN I WAS A CHILD, OBO-SAN. I AM WHAT I AM TODAY BECAUSE OF YOUR GENEROSITY.

I GRIEVE BECAUSE NAYAPO HAS LOST AN HONORED SON AND A TRUE HERO.

YOUR CONCERN IS MOST KIND, OBO-SAN...

...BUT I AM ACCUSTOMED TO HIDING MY FEELINGS.

BUT YOU AND TODOSI WERE...

...CLOSE.

YOUR GRIEF IS KEENER THAN MOST WOULD KNOW.

OF COURSE.

OBO-SAN...

...*YOUR* BROTHER'S DEATH IS *MY* BROTHER'S DEATH.

TODOSI WAS NOT ONLY MY LOYAL SERVANT, BUT A LOYAL SERVANT TO *ALL* NAYADO.

PLEASE...

...HONOR YOUR BROTHER BY GUIDING HIS JOURNEY TO THE PURE LAND.

I WILL NOT DO THIS THING.

WHAT IS *THIS?*

I WILL NOT ENGAGE IN A FALSE RITUAL TO FALSE GODS.

...AND I WILL USE THE GODS' OWN WEAPON TO **DESTROY** THEM!

HERESY.

MY BROTHER'S SPIRIT WILL INDEED JOURNEY TO THE PURE LAND...

...BUT NOT WITH THE BLESSING OF FALSE GODS.

YOUR BROTHER'S **BLOOD** PAID FOR IT. DO NOT LET HIS SACRIFICE BE FOR NOTHING.

THE WEAPON IS THE MEANS OF OUR VICTORY OVER SHINACEA. FINALLY, WE HOLD POWER ENOUGH TO **ANNIHILATE** OUR ENEMIES.

I AM SORRY, MY EMPEROR. YOU ASK THAT WHICH I CANNOT DO.

I CANNOT SURRENDER THE WEAPON.

GIVE ME THE WEAPON.

OBO-SAN. *GIVE ME THE WEAPON.*

YOU *DENY* MY WILL?

DO NOT PRESUME OUR PAST FRIENDSHIP GRANTS YOU LEAVE TO IGNORE YOUR EMPEROR, OBO-SAN.

GIVE ME THE WEAPON!

I MUST REFUSE.

TO PROVOKE SHINACEA AGAIN IS MADNESS.

MY GODS HAVE BETRAYED ME. I WILL NOT ALLOW MY NATION TO DO THE *SAME* TO HER PEOPLE.

HOW *DARE* YOU *DEFY* ME! *GENERAL RYUICHI!*

THE PATH • CHAPTER TWO

OBO-SAN...

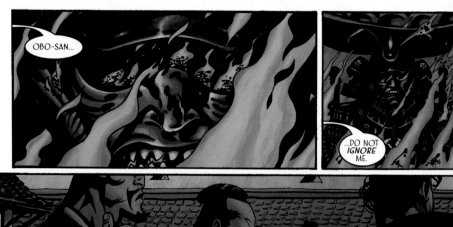

OBO-SAN...

...DO NOT *IGNORE* ME.

NOW TAKE UP THIS BLADE AND CUT OPEN YOUR BELLY! *I DEMAND IT!*

MITSUMUNE...

...YOU MUST LISTEN TO ME.

YOU *MUST*.

YOU *DARE* DEFY...

...YOU WILL *DESTROY* NAYADO.

OUR EMPEROR *MUST* RETURN. CONQUER THIS MADNESS WITHIN YOU, MITSUMUNE, OR ALL WILL BE LOST.

DO YOU *UNDERSTAND?*

WHAT HAVE I *DONE?*

I *KILLED* HIM.

IT'S NOT TOO LATE, MITSUMUNE.

YOU CAN STILL MAKE—

NO.

NO, OBO-SAN....

I KNOW YOU OF OLD, AND YOU ARE *CHANGED*.

YOUR DECISIONS ARE NOT THOSE OF THE MAN WHO WAS MY FRIEND.

NOT THOSE OF A *RATIONAL* MAN.

I KNOW NOT WHAT OR WHY, BUT SOME *MALADY* ASSAILS YOUR MIND.

IF YOU DO NOT COME TO YOUR SENSES, OUR NATION WILL SUFFER THE PRICE. IF YOU DO NOT *TURN* FROM THIS PATH...

THE MARK.

YES.

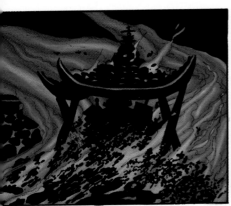

I KILLED THEM *ALL*.

NAYADO IS MINE TO SAFEGUARD...

...AND I NEARLY LED IT TO *RUIN*.

...THERE IS *NO FORGIVENESS* FOR WHAT I'VE DONE.

RYUICHI...

71

IS THIS WHAT YOU WANTED? *IS IT?*

TO PLACE NOT ONLY YOUR *BROTHER* UPON A PYRE, BUT YOUR *EMPEROR* AS WELL?

WHAT DID YOU *DO* TO HIM, OBO-SAN?

THERE IS NO *HEIR* TO THE THRONE, OBO-SAN. NAYADO WILL BE PLUNGED INTO *CHAOS.*

HOW MANY CLANS WILL CHALLENGE THE OHIRAS FOR THE THRONE? SIX? EIGHT? *A DOZEN?*

WE NEED WORRY ABOUT *SHINACEA* NO LONGER.

WE WILL DESTROY *OURSELVES.*

ah

...TAKE HIM.

IS IT SO EASY TO BRAND ME A TRAITOR, RYUICHI? *YOUR* LOYALTY IS TO THE THRONE.

MINE IS TO MY *NATION.*

DOWN.

OBO-SAN...

...AIKO HAS RETURNED.

WE NEED TO BE GOING. THE WEATHER'S GOING TO TURN.

SHOULD I ASK WHERE YOU GOT THE HORSES, AIKO?

...NOT IF YOU DON'T WANT TO HEAR THE *ANSWER*.

I AM INDEBTED TO BOTH YOU AND WULF FOR YOUR DEEDS ON MY BEHALF...

THE DEPTH OF FEELING FOR YOU IS MUCH THE SAME AS IT WAS FOR YOUR BROTHER.

OBO-SAN, WHAT OF MITSUMUNE?

WE ALL SAW IT, YET HOW IS THIS THING THAT HAPPENED *POSSIBLE?*

NO...

...FOR WHAT YOU HAVE *SUFFERED*...

...BUT YOU NEED NOT DO THIS.

LET THIS *DEATH SENTENCE* BE MINE ALONE.

OUR FATES AND YOURS ARE NOW THE *SAME*. NOTHING CAN CHANGE THAT.

WE SWORE OUR LOYALTY TO TODOSI...

...THAT VOW EXTENDS TO *YOU*.

I COULD NOT EXPLAIN THE MADNESS THAT GRIPPED HIM. THIS...

RESURRECTION...

...I CANNOT EVEN *BEGIN* TO UNDERSTAND.

WHERE DO WE GO NOW?

MY MONASTERY IN THE NORTH. WE'LL BE *SAFE* THERE...

...FOR A TIME.

AND AFTER THAT?

AFTER THAT?

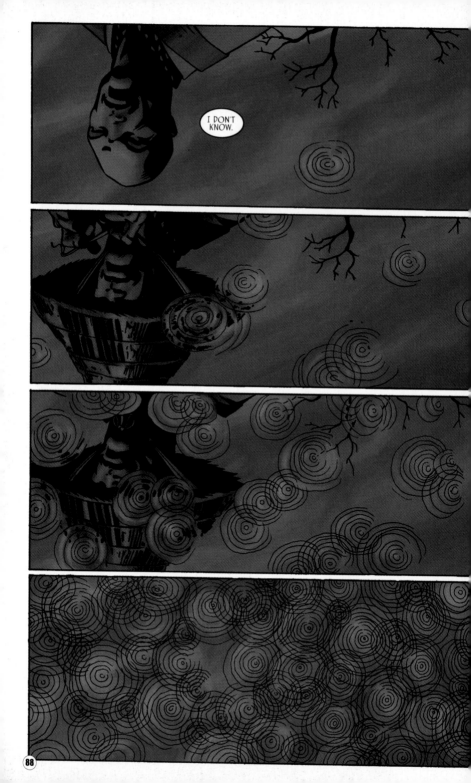

"BRING ME MY *GENERAL*."

YOU SUMMONED ME, MY LORD?

THE REST OF YOU...

...*LEAVE US*.

I WOULD SPEAK TO MY GENERAL IN PRIVATE.

RYUICHI...

WE GREW TO MANHOOD TOGETHER, DID WE NOT, RYUICHI?

YOU.

ME.

TODOSI.

OBO-SAN.

AND WE HAVE COME TO *THIS*.

TODOSI IS DEAD, AND OBO-SAN HAS FLED IN *DEFIANCE* OF MY WILL.

I SEE OBO-SAN AT LEAST LEFT YOU SOMETHING TO *REMEMBER* HIM BY.

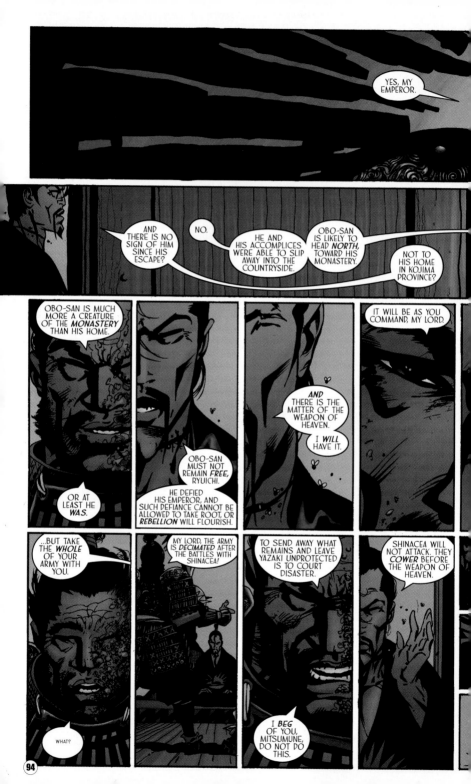

YES, MY EMPEROR.

AND THERE IS NO SIGN OF HIM SINCE HIS ESCAPE?

NO.

HE AND HIS ACCOMPLICES WERE ABLE TO SLIP AWAY INTO THE COUNTRYSIDE.

OBO-SAN IS LIKELY TO HEAD *NORTH*, TOWARD HIS MONASTERY.

NOT TO HIS HOME IN KOJIMA PROVINCE?

OBO-SAN IS MUCH MORE A CREATURE OF THE *MONASTERY* THAN HIS HOME.

OR AT LEAST HE *WAS.*

OBO-SAN MUST NOT REMAIN *FREE,* RYUICHI.

HE DEFIED HIS EMPEROR, AND SUCH DEFIANCE CANNOT BE ALLOWED TO TAKE ROOT, OR *REBELLION* WILL FLOURISH.

AND THERE IS THE MATTER OF THE WEAPON OF HEAVEN.

I *WILL* HAVE IT.

IT WILL BE AS YOU COMMAND, MY LORD.

...BUT TAKE THE *WHOLE* OF YOUR ARMY WITH YOU.

WHAT?

MY LORD, THE ARMY IS *DECIMATED* AFTER THE BATTLES WITH SHINACEA!

TO SEND AWAY WHAT REMAINS AND LEAVE YAZAKI UNPROTECTED IS TO COURT DISASTER.

I *BEG* OF YOU, MITSUMUNE, DO NOT DO THIS.

SHINACEA WILL NOT ATTACK. THEY *COWER* BEFORE THE WEAPON OF HEAVEN.

94

THEY'LL SEND RYUICHI AFTER US.

THEY'RE PROBABLY HARD ON OUR TRAIL ALREADY.

AND RYUICHI KNOWS ME WELL ENOUGH TO KNOW WHERE WE'RE HEADED.

AND I BELIEVE *YOU* GAVE HIM ADDED INCENTIVE TO FIND US, WULF.

AND WHAT WOULD YOU HAVE HAD ME DO?

LET HIM CUT YOU DOWN, OBO-SAN?

WHY DO WE MAKE FOR YOUR MONASTERY, OBO-SAN, IF RYUICHI ALREADY KNOWS IT IS OUR DESTINATION?

WILL WE NOT BE BETTER SERVED FINDING REFUGE ELSEWHERE?

YOU *KNOW* WHAT THEY'LL DO.

I DO NOT BELIEVE HE WOULD HAVE DONE SO.

YOU THINK HE WOULD HAVE STAYED HIS HAND SIMPLY BECAUSE YOU WERE *FRIENDS* AS BOYS?

MITSUMUNE WAS YOUR BOYHOOD FRIEND AS WELL, AND IT'S *HE* WHO ORDERED YOUR EXECUTION.

RYUICHI IS MITSUMUNE'S CREATURE, OBO-SAN...

...*WHATEVER* MITSUMUNE HAS BECOME.

DON'T CONCERN YOURSELF, WULF.

THERE *IS* NO BETTER REFUGE.

OBO-SAN?

THE MONASTERY WILL SERVE ITS PURPOSE.

IS IT THE **WEAPON** THAT WILL PROTECT US, OBO-SAN?

IS **THAT** WHAT YOU INTEND?

I USED THE WEAPON OF HEAVEN TO BANISH THE GODS FROM THE BATTLEFIELD.

BUT I UNDERSTAND **LITTLE** OF IT BEYOND THAT.

I DON'T KNOW IF IT EVEN **COULD** BE USED FOR THE PURPOSES MITSUMUNE WISHES.

SOON WE WON'T BE SO LUCKY.

WHEN WORD OF THE PRICE ON OUR HEADS **SPREADS**...

...**EVERYONE** WILL BE AN ENEMY.

UNFORTUNATELY TRUE.

OBO-SAN, WHAT OF THE **MARK** THE GODS GRANTED YOU?

IT APPEARS WE ARE NOT ALONE ON THIS ROAD.

NO.

THE MARK WAS GRANTED TO *TODOSI*, AND PASSED TO ME.

DID YOU KNOW IT *GLOWED* WHEN YOU SPOKE TO MITSUMUNE? IT WAS VISIBLE EVEN THROUGH YOUR ROBES.

THE MARK... GLOWED?

I ONLY KNOW IT FELT AS THOUGH THE *TRUE* MITSUMUNE WAS LOOKING AT ME THEN.

THE TRUE MITSUMUNE WHO TOOK HIS OWN LIFE. MORE THAN THAT, I—

OBO-SAN, WULF...

IT IS NOTHING I WANTED *THEN*. NOTHING I WANT *NOW*.

COULD *IT* HAVE BREATHED LIFE BACK INTO HIM?

I DO NOT BELIEVE IT PLAYED A PART IN THE RESURRECTION, BUT I CANNOT BE SURE.

...A SHRINE.

AS GOOD A PLACE AS ANY TO REST THE HORSES.

A BUILDING TO YOU. TO ME, IT IS THE *LIE* UPON WHICH I BUILT MY LIFE.

MY BROTHER DEDICATED HIMSELF TO A MARTIAL EXISTENCE, BECAUSE HE BELIEVED IT WAS THE BEST WAY TO SERVE NAYADO.

I GAVE MY LIFE OVER TO RELIGION, BECAUSE I BELIEVED IN ITS IDEALS. AND BECAUSE I BELIEVED MY PIETY SERVED NAYADO IN ITS OWN WAY.

MY *FAITH* WAS THE ENTIRETY OF MY BEING, WULF.

AND THEN THE GODS FORSOOK ME.

OBO-SAN? I KNOW IN MANY WAYS YOU MUST FEEL...

...ABANDONED.

I UNDERSTAND WHAT THAT IS. AS A GIRL *I* WAS ABANDONED WHEN MY PARENTS, MY WHOLE VILLAGE, SUCCUMBED TO THE SICKNESS.

I HAD NOWHERE TO GO.

BUT WHEN I FELT MOST LOST AN *ANSWER* PRESENTED ITSELF.

YOUR FAMILY TOOK ME IN. THE TSUGAWAS GAVE ME A CHANCE FOR MY LIFE TO HAVE MEANING AND PURPOSE AGAIN.

THERE IS A *PATH* FOR YOU, OBO-SAN.

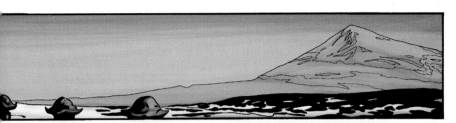

OBO-SAN? ARE YOU COMING DOWN?

I AM *FINISHED* WITH THESE GODS AND ALL THEIR TRAPPINGS.

IT'S JUST A *BUILDING,* OBO-SAN.

OR MORE TRULY, I FORSOOK *THEM* WHEN I SAW THEM FOR THE PETTY BEINGS THEY TRULY ARE.

I WILL HAVE NOTHING MORE TO DO WITH THEM...

...SAVE TO HAVE MY *VENGEANCE* UPON THEM.

SUIT YOURSELF.

I'M THIRSTY.

AND YOU NEED NOT WALK IT ALONE.

THERE ARE OTHERS WHO WILL JOIN YOU...

...WHEREVER YOU DECIDE YOUR PATH LEADS.

WULF WILL STAND WITH YOU.

I WILL STAND WITH YOU.

BANDITS!

HAA!

GHLK!

HRRGH...

WHICH OF YOU FIRST?

UNNNHH

GYAAH

AIKO?

I'M FINE.

THANK YOU.

IT'S THE *MARK*, OBO-SAN. THE *MARK* ALLOWED YOU TO DO THAT.

YOU ASKED MITSUMUNE TO SEE THE TRUTH, AND HE *DID*.

YOU TOLD THE BANDIT *"STOP,"* AND HE *DID*.

...SEEKING REFUGE IN A *MONASTERY?*

I HOPE HE'S AT LEAST ABLE TO GAIN SOME MEASURE OF PEACE THERE, HOWEVER FLEETING.

AND *THEN?*

I FEAR WHAT THE FUTURE HOLDS FOR HIM, WULF.

IT IS AS I SAID BEFORE, AIKO.

HE IS *LOST.*

THEN WE NEED TO HELP HIM FIND HIS WAY.

HE HASN'T SPOKEN SINCE WE LEFT THE SHRINE.

HE'S BURIED HIS BROTHER AND CAST ASIDE HIS FAITH.

HE IS BRANDED WITH THE MARK OF THOSE HE HATES.

HOW COULD HIS MIND BE ANYTHING *BUT* TURMOIL?

OBO-SAN'S VERY *BEING* IS CONFLICTED. HOW ELSE DO YOU EXPLAIN A MAN WHO HAS FORSWORN HIS RELIGION...

OBO-SAN?

WE'VE ARRIVED.

THAT?

Oh, I THINK *THAT* WILL DO NICELY.

"...I HAVE *FRIENDS* THERE."

OBO-SAN!

THE MONASTERY IS NEVER THE SAME WHEN YOU LEAVE ON YOUR TRAVELS, OBO-SAN.

WE ARE RICHER FOR YOUR RETURN.

AIKO? YOU HAVE BEEN TO THIS PLACE BEFORE?

UPON OCCASION, WULF.

WHEN OBO-SAN JOINED THE ORDER, HE USED PART OF THE TSUGAWA FORTUNE TO CONSTRUCT TAKAIHASHI MONASTERY.

HE IS WELL LOVED BY HIS FELLOW MONKS HERE.

THIS IS THE WEAPON OF HEAVEN. I CLAIMED IT UPON THE BATTLEFIELD WHERE MY BROTHER PERISHED DEFENDING NAYADO FROM SHINACEA'S HORDES.

I CLAIMED IT FROM *GODS* WHO HAD TURNED THEIR BACKS UPON OUR CAUSE. WORSE, THEY HAD *SPORT* WITH US.

I HAVE SEEN THE TRUE FACE OF THE GODS AND MY FAITH IS NO MORE.

I HAVE VOWED TO *DESTROY* THEM FOR THEIR PERFIDY.

AND *THIS* WILL BE THE INSTRUMENT OF THAT DESTRUCTION.

IN THE TIME SINCE, I RETURNED TO YAZAKI FOR MY BROTHER'S FUNERAL.

THERE EMPEROR MITSUMUNE DEMANDED THE WEAPON FROM ME, BUT I REFUSED HIM BECAUSE I BELIEVE HIM TO BE *MAD*.

MITSUMUNE TOOK HIS OWN LIFE...

...BUT WAS *RESURRECTED* AND CALLED FOR MY *EXECUTION*.

I ESCAPED ONLY WITH THE HELP OF WULF AND AIKO, THEN CAME HERE.

118

I WONDER IF THEY WILL BE SO WELCOMING ONCE THEY LEARN WHAT OBO-SAN BRINGS DOWN UPON THEM.

YOUR PRESENCE SHOWERS *PEACE* UPON THESE WALLS.

PERHAPS NOT, KONOSKE-SAN.

I THANK YOU FOR YOUR RECEPTION, MY BROTHERS. THIS IS INDEED HOME TO ME...

...BUT I FEAR I'VE BROUGHT *ILL FORTUNE* TO OUR WALLS.

I FEEL CERTAIN GENERAL RYUICHI WILL SEEK ME, WITH HIS WARRIORS IN TOW, BUT I KNEW OF NOWHERE ELSE I COULD FIND SANCTUARY.

MY BROTHERS, I BEG YOUR FORGIVENESS.

YOU ARE *ONE* OF US, OBO-SAN. *YOUR* TRIALS ARE *OUR* TRIALS.

WE WILL NEVER *ABANDON* YOU.

YOU AND YOUR FRIENDS ARE WELCOME HERE WHETHER YOU BRING GOOD FORTUNE OR ILL.

WE WILL MAKE THE *NECESSARY* PREPARATIONS.

THANK YOU, I—

Uh?

OBO-SAN!

OBO-SAN!

WULF!
WULF!
WULF!

Uh...

...NO, THAT'S ALL RIGHT.

WULF.

OBO-SAN...?

THIS IS KATAYAMA SOJIROU.

HE IS NEWLY ARRIVED FROM TANAKA PROVINCE IN THE SOUTH.

I AM PLEASED TO MEET YOU, OBO-SAN.

I CAME HERE *HOPING* I WOULD HAVE A CHANCE TO DO SO.

TRULY?

WHY SO, SOJIROU-SAN?

YOU SAY YOU HAVE LOST YOUR FAITH...

...YET YOU CAME *HERE*.

CURIOUS, IS IT NOT?

I DID NOT KNOW WHERE ELSE TO GO.

THIS MONASTERY HAS BEEN FAR MORE OF A HOME TO ME THAN ANY OTHER PLACE. OUR ORDER HAS BEEN THE CENTER OF MY EXISTENCE.

JUST AS SAMURAI TRADITION AND THE WAYS OF WAR GAVE SHAPE TO MY BROTHER'S LIFE, MY DEVOTION TO THE GODS GAVE *MY* LIFE SHAPE.

I SAW THEIR HAND IN THE NATURAL ORDER AND BEAUTY OF THE WORLD.

ONCE I WOULD HAVE SEEN THIS AS A REFLECTION OF *DIVINE HARMONY*.

NOW IT IS MERELY A *POND*.

THE GODS REVEALED THEIR TRUE NATURE TO ME, AND *THEY* ARE NOT AS I ONCE SAW THEM.

THEY ARE *FALSE*.

YOU FEEL *BETRAYED*.

HAVE YOU CONSIDERED THAT PERHAPS IT IS NOT THE *GODS* THAT ARE FALSE, BUT YOUR *BELIEFS*?

THAT PERHAPS THOSE YOU THOUGHT OF AS GODS ARE NOT GODS AT ALL...

...BUT BEINGS JUST AS FALLIBLE AS *MEN?*

NOW WHOSE ACTIONS SEEM CURIOUS?

IS NOT SUCH A STATEMENT *BLASPHEMOUS* COMING FROM A MONK OF OUR ORDER?

WE ARE INFINITELY MORE POWERFUL THAN THESE FISH THAT SWIM IN THE POND. THEIR EXISTENCE IS AT OUR WHIM.

BUT THAT DOES NOT MAKE US *GODS*.

TELL ME OF THE *MARK* YOU BEAR.

HOW CAN *YOU* KNOW OF IT? I DID NOT MENTION IT WITHIN.

I KNOW *MANY* THINGS.

IT...GIVES ME A POWER.

DIFFERENT THAN THE MIGHT IT GAVE MY BROTHER UPON THE FIELD OF BATTLE.

ON THE JOURNEY HERE WE WERE ACCOSTED BY BANDITS. I COMMANDED ONE OF THEM TO *STOP,* AND HE DID.

HE COULD NOT DISOBEY MY WILL.

IT'S NOT THE *POWER* I QUESTION. I QUESTION WHAT YOU WILL *DO* WITH IT.

YOU CANNOT HIDE HERE FOREVER.

NO

YOU SPEAK OF *REVENGE* AGAINST THE GODS, OBO-SAN. BUT HOW WILL YOU ACCOMPLISH SUCH A THING?

WHERE WILL YOU *FIND* THESE "GODS" TO PUNISH THEM?

PERHAPS YOUR CONCERNS SHOULD BE OF A MORE *EARTHLY* NATURE.

SO THEN, WHAT WILL YOU *DO?*

WHAT HAS BEEN PUT IN MOTION WILL NOT *EASILY* BE PUT TO REST.

EASIER TO CATCH *SMOKE...*

...SET ADRIFT ON THE AIR.

YOU BELIEVE THE EMPEROR IS *MAD*, DO YOU NOT?

THAT MITSUMUNE IS NOT THE SAME MAN YOU KNEW, ESPECIALLY AFTER HIS RESURRECTION?

YOU MUST DECIDE WHETHER YOU WILL STAND IDLE WHILE HE CONTINUES PLACING NAYADO AT RISK...

...OR IF YOU HAVE THE COURAGE TO USE YOUR GIFTS TO *TOPPLE* MITSUMUNE.

FORGIVE ME FOR INTERRUPTING, OBO-SAN...

...BUT RYUICHI HAS ARRIVED.

I *SEE*, YET I STILL DO NOT BELIEVE. THE ENTIRETY OF NAYADO'S ARMY ARRAYED BEFORE US...

...MEANING YAZAKI STAND UNPROTECTED.

MITSUMUNE TRULY *MUST* BE MAD.

LOOK THERE...

...RYUICHI HIMSELF, UNDER A FLAG OF TRUCE.

SUCH A FORCE COULD *EASILY* OVERWHELM US. WHY DOES RYUICHI NOT ATTACK?

OBO-SAN, YOU'RE NOT *GOING* TO HIM, ARE YOU?

HOW ELSE WILL I KNOW WHAT HE WANTS?

BUT HE TRIED TO *KILL* YOU.

TRUE...

...BUT HE DID NOT SUCCEED.

RYUICHI.

OBO-SAN.

YOU *KNOW* WHY I AM HERE.

THE EMPEROR HAS SENT ME TO RETRIEVE THE WEAPON OF HEAVEN. *AND* YOUR HEAD.

WHY WOULD MITSUMUNE NEED *MY* HEAD, WHEN HE HAS ONE OF HIS *OWN* HE SO RECENTLY BECAME ATTACHED TO?

MY APOLOGIES FOR THE INJURIES YOU SUFFERED.

IT WAS NOT MY INTENT.

I APPRECIATE YOUR CONCERN.

SO TO WHAT DO I OWE THE PLEASURE OF YOUR VISIT?

PLEASE DO NOT MAKE THIS MORE DIFFICULT THAN IT NEED BE, OBO-SAN.

WILL YOU *SIT?*

MUST YOU MAKE LIGHT, OBO-SAN?

ONCE YOU WERE TSUGAWA NOBUYUKI. WE WERE AS BROTHERS WHEN WE WERE BOYS.

YOU WERE RAISED IN THE SAMURAI WAY, AS WAS YOUR *BROTHER*, AS WAS *I.* YOU UNDERSTAND *HONOR...*

...AND YOU UNDERSTAND MY HONOR IS DEARER TO ME THAN MY OWN LIFE. HONOR DEMANDS I FULFILL MY DUTY TO MY EMPEROR.

SURRENDER THE WEAPON OF HEAVEN TO ME.

I REFUSED YOUR REQUEST AT YAZAKI.

I MUST REFUSE NOW.

OBO-SAN...

...IF YOU GIVE ME THE WEAPON I WILL ALLOW YOU TO *FLEE*.

YOU NEED NEVER BE *SEEN* AGAIN.

I WILL RETURN TO MITSUMUNE...

THEN YOU LEAVE ME WITH NO CHOICE BUT TO *TAKE* THE WEAPON.

DO YOU *SEE* THE ARMY AT MY BACK, OBO-SAN?

YOU BRING YOUR *DOOM* UPON YOURSELF AND ALL WITHIN.

YOU FORCE ME TO GIVE THE ORDER AND *MARCH* UPON YOUR MONASTERY.

YOU WI... WHAT MUS...

AS WILL ...

...I WILL TELL HIM YOU WERE *SLAIN* AND YOUR BODY LOST.

I AM OFFERING YOU YOUR *LIFE*, OBO-SAN, AND THOSE OF ALL YOUR COMPANIONS...

...IF ONLY YOU WILL SURRENDER THE WEAPON.

I CANNOT.

TO DO SO WOULD BE TO GIVE A MADMAN THE TOOL TO DESTROY OUR NATION.

WHY MUST YOU BE THIS WAY?!

DOES *HONOR* MEAN NOTHING TO YOU?

LOYALTY?

I MUST DO AS MY HEART WILLS AND MY CONSCIENCE DICTATES.

I MUST DO WHAT I BELIEVE IS BEST FOR NAYADO.

GOODBYE, RYUICHI.

I AM *PAINED* THAT IT MUST BE SO.

AND *I* AM PAINED THAT WE ARE BROUGHT TO THIS OVER A SCRAP OF METAL NO BIGGER THAN A CHILD'S BLADE.

MY OLD FRIEND...

...IS *THAT* ALL YOU BELIEVE THIS IS ABOUT?

FOOL.

READY THE TROOPS!

131

HE'S MADE HIS CHOICE.

PREPARE TO LAY SIEGE.

FOR *THIS* YOU INTERRUPT MY RETREAT?

I TOLD YOU TO BRING ME THE *WEAPON OF HEAVEN*...

...AND INSTEAD YOU DELIVER A DEAD MAN'S *SKULL*.

YOU HAVE BEEN USEFUL TO ME IN THE PAST, YUKIO...

YES, YES, I SUPPOSE.

GREAT SHINACEA AGAIN FINDS ITSELF PRESENTED WITH OPPORTUNITIES...

...OPPORTUNITIES TO *DEVOUR* NAYADO.

MITSUMUNE'S *RESURRECTION* IS DISQUIETING, BUT THAT CAN BE DEALT WITH IN ITS OWN TIME.

I THINK, PERHAPS, MATTERS HAVE WORKED OUT *BEST* THIS WAY.

THE MONK ESCAPES WITH THE WEAPON OF HEAVEN...

YOU WILL GO TO THE MONASTERY FOR ME, YUKIO, AND YOU WILL TAKE THE WEAPON OF HEAVEN FROM THIS MONK.

BRING *OTHERS* IF YOU MUST.

YOU CAN *DO* THIS?

"...RYUICHI STILL SLEEPS."

ANYTHING?

NO...

YOU REALIZE DESTROYING THE *BRIDGE* WON'T STOP RYUICHI'S ARMY FOR LONG, OBO-SAN.

HIS ARMY MUST OUTNUMBER THE MONKS WITHIN THE MONASTERY TEN TO ONE.

...YOURS *OR* AIKO'S.

AND *I* HAVE TOLD YOU BEFORE, MY LOYALTY *WAS* TO YOUR BROTHER, *NOW* IT IS TO YOU.

I STAY.

WHAT *WAS* IT BETWEEN YOU AND TODOSI? HE NEVER SHARED THE WHOLE OF THE TALE WITH ME WHEN HE BROUGHT YOU TO OUR HOME.

THEY'LL START FELLING TREES TO MAKE LAUNCHES.

THEY *WILL* REACH THE ISLAND.

THAT IS LIKELY SO.

IT IS *ABSOLUTELY* SO.

RYUICHI OFFERED TO SPARE YOU AND YOU REFUSED HIM. NOW THERE IS NO OTHER PATH FOR HIM TO TAKE.

RYUICHI IS THE EMPEROR'S TOOL...

...AND HE WILL PLACE HIS *DUTY* ABOVE ALL ELSE. *INCLUDING* YOUR FRIENDSHIP.

I IMAGINE THE NUMBER IS CLOSER TO TWENTY.

JEST IF YOU WILL, OBO-SAN.

THIS WILL END IN BLOOD AND DEATH.

IT NEED NOT END IN *YOUR* DEATH, WULF...

I HAVE TOLD YOU BEFORE, THIS IS NOT YOUR BATTLE.

YOU AND AIKO COULD STEAL AWAY FROM THE MONASTERY...

...AND BE *GONE* BEFORE WHAT IS TO COME.

YOUR BROTHER GAVE ME MY *LIFE*.

MY PEOPLE HAIL FROM THE OTHER SIDE OF THE WORLD...

...A NORTHLAND OF HARSH MOUNTAINS AND FJORDS...

WE ARE SEA ROVERS, TAKING WHAT WE WOULD AND FACING WHAT DANGERS THE SEA WOULD PLACE IN OUR PATH.

MINE WAS A PROUD CLAN.

LEADERSHIP PASSED TO THE ELDEST, MY BROTHER JARL. I STOOD AT HIS SIDE WHILE HE LED US ON OUR RAIDS IN LONGSHIPS CROWNED WITH FIERCE CARVINGS.

...WHERE WE PRAY TO WILD GODS...

...AND LIVE IN VILLAGES CARVED FROM THE ROCKY SHORES.

WHEN I WAS BARELY A MAN, MY FATHER DIED IN BATTLE, AS BEFITS A WARRIOR, THE BODIES OF HIS ENEMIES PILED AT HIS FEET.

UPON ONE OF OUR JOURNEYS WE SACKED AND BURNED A RIVAL'S CASTLE...

...A FORTRESS MY PEOPLE HAD BEEN UNABLE TO CONQUER SINCE THE TIME OF MY FATHER'S FATHER'S FATHER.

FEW HAD EVER STOOD AGAINST MY BROTHER, WHO WAS TRULY AMONG THE MIGHTIEST OF OUR PEOPLE.

HE STRUCK DOWN THE PRINCE AND KEPT THE WOMAN FOR HIMSELF.

INSTEAD, HE BANISHED JARL FROM OUR HOMELAND, VOWING HIS DEATH SHOULD HE RETURN.

I PLEDGED MY LOYALTY TO MY BROTHER, AS DID MANY OF THOSE WHO HAD PLUNDERED WITH HIM, AND WE SAILED FROM OUR HOME WITH THE WIND AT OUR BACKS.

OUR JOURNEY WAS THE STUFF OF EPIC POEM, BUT WE HAD NONE SAVE OURSELVES TO LISTEN TO THE TALE.

WE TRAVERSED STRANGE SEAS WHERE SAVAGE STORMS BATTERED US. LORRIDE, WHO HAD BEEN THE START OF IT ALL, WAS SWEPT OVERBOARD AND LOST.

WHEN THE SEA CALMED, WE FOUND OURSELVES ADRIFT, MORE DISTANT FROM OUR HOMELAND THAN ANY OF MY PEOPLE HAD EVER SAILED.

WE MET THEM WITH SWORDS DRAWN, BUT WE COULD NOT WITHSTAND THEIR ATTACK. EVEN OUR SHIELD WALL WAS BROKEN.

...YET SOON ONLY MY BROTHER AND I STILL DREW BREATH.

DESPITE MY OWN WOUNDS, I CUT MY WAY TO THE NOGAWA'S MOUNT AND FLED.

BUT I WOULD DIE IN A PLACE OF MY CHOOSING, A NARROW PLACE WHERE MY ATTACKERS COULD ONLY COME AT ME SINGLY. A PLACE WHERE MY BLADE WOULD DRINK LONG AND DEEP.

I KNOW NOW OUR ATTACKERS WERE OF THE NOGAWA CLAN, UPON WHOSE TERRITORY WE HAD LANDED. HE WHO LED THEM DISMOUNTED AND FOUGHT JARL, SHATTERING MY BROTHER'S BLADE AND SLAYING HIM.

I WAS NOT MOVED BY COWARDICE. I DID NOT FEAR DEATH, AND INDEED I DID INTEND TO DIE THAT DAY.

I WOULD AVENGE MY BROTHER, AND THEN DIE AS HE AND MY FATHER HAD, PASSING INTO THE ALL-FATHER'S HALL WITH MY ENEMIES PILED AT MY FEET.

THE NOGAWAS ADVANCED AND I SLEW EACH ONE AS HE CAME.

THEY FOUND A WAY TO ATTACK ME SO THAT I FACED TWO BLADES AT ONCE.

I SAW MY DEATH WAS LIKELY UPON ME...

...AND REGRETTED ONLY THAT I WOULD BE UNABLE TO HAVE MY VENGEANCE UPON JARL'S SLAYER.

MY SAVIOR ARRIVED ON HORSEBACK, LOOSING A FLURRY OF ARROWS THAT TOOK MOST OF THE NOGAWAS. YOUR BROTHER, OF COURSE.

I DID NOT UNDERSTAND WHY I HAD BEEN SAVED AT THE TIME, I SAW NOTHING TO INDICATE TODOSI WAS ANY DIFFERENT THAN THOSE WHO HAD ATTACKED ME.

THE NOGAWA CLEAVED MY BLADE, AS I EXPECTED HIM TO...

...BUT I DREW HIM CLOSE...

But rescue came in the form of an arrow that felled one of my attackers, nearly splitting his skull.

I thought perhaps he had simply taken the side of the underdog, and that was true...

...but it was more the long-standing animosity between your family and the Nogawas that had spared me.

My brother's killer faced me. My blade was no match for his *dotanuki*, this I knew.

...and drove the shattered remainder through a seam in his armor.

Your brother had allowed me to avenge my own.

WE HAD NO COMMON TONGUE, YET WE RECOGNIZED IN EACH OTHER A FELLOW WARRIOR OF HONOR.

IN SILENCE, HE HELPED ME GATHER MY DEAD AND PLACE THEM IN OUR LONGBOAT...

HE TOOK ME TO KOJIMA...

...TO THE ESTATE OF YOUR FAMILY...

...AND TAUGHT ME YOUR LANGUAGE, YOUR CUSTOMS, THE WAYS OF THE WARRIORS OF NAYADO.

HE SHARED THESE THINGS WITH ME, EVEN THOUGH HE HAD NO REASON TO DO SO.

ON THE BATTLEFIELD, HIS DECISION WAS NEVER QUESTIONED. TO STAND BESIDE TODOSI WAS TO HAVE MY OWN BROTHER AT MY BACK. ALL OF NAYADO' ENEMIES FELL TO OUR BLADES.

154

...AND THEN, AS IS OUR CUSTOM, SET IT TO SEA ABLAZE.

I WAS ALONE IN A LAND STRANGER THAN ANY I COULD HAVE IMAGINED, BUT TODOSI GAVE ME A HOME.

TODOSI SCHOOLED ME UNTIL I WAS ABLE TO DUEL HIM TO A DRAW, HIS SPEED COUNTERED BY MY STRENGTH.

OR THAT IS WHAT HE LED ME TO BELIEVE.

HE PRESENTED ME WITH MY ARMOR AND SWORD AND NAMED ME HIS LIEUTENANT, IGNORING THE SCANDAL CAUSED BY NAYADO'S WARLORD SO ENTRUSTING A BARBARIAN.

THUS DID I BECOME SAMURAI.

I HAD INTENDED TO *DIE* THE DAY I MET YOUR BROTHER AND BURIED MY OWN.

PERHAPS I *DID*...

...FOR I WAS *REBORN* AS YOU SEE ME NOW.

THIS LIFE WAS GIVEN TO ME BY TODOSI.

NOW THAT HE IS GONE, ALL THAT I OWE TO *HIM* I OWE TO *YOU.*

LOYALTY TO *MY* BROTHER LED ME TO THESE SHORES.

LOYALTY TO *YOUR* BROTHER LED ME TO THIS CAUSE.

AND MY LOYALTY TO *YOU* WILL KEEP ME HERE AS LONG AS I DRAW BREATH, OBO-SAN.

WHATEVER IS TO COME.

YOUR SATCHEL COULD WELL HOLD THE MEANS TO OUR VICTORY. YOU *KNOW* THAT.

RYUICHI'S ARMY IS SIZABLE...

...BUT I DOUBT IT COULD WITHSTAND WHAT YOU POSSESS.

TRUE...

...THE WEAPON OF HEAVEN LIKELY COMMANDS ENOUGH MIGHT TO *DRIVE AWAY* RYUICHI.

PERHAPS EVEN TO DESTROY HIM.

BUT I WILL NOT USE IT AGAINST NAYADO'S SONS.

IT IS A FOUL THING OF EVIL GODS. I SAID IT WILL BE USED ONLY AGAINST *THEM*, AND I WILL HOLD TO MY VOW.

OBO-SAN!

AWAY WITH YOU...

...DAMNED CARRION EATER.

MY PEOPLE BELIEVE SUCH BIRDS ARE AN ILL OMEN, OBO-SAN. DO NOT IGNORE PORTENTS WHEN THEY PRESENT THEMSELVES.

YOU FORGET, WULF...

...I NO LONGER BELIEVE IN *ANYTHING*.

APPARENTLY RYUICHI HAS AWAKENED.

APPARENTLY.

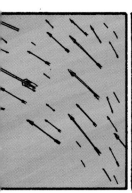

AT LEAST WE ARE SAFE BEHIND THE MONASTERY WALLS.

FOR NOW.

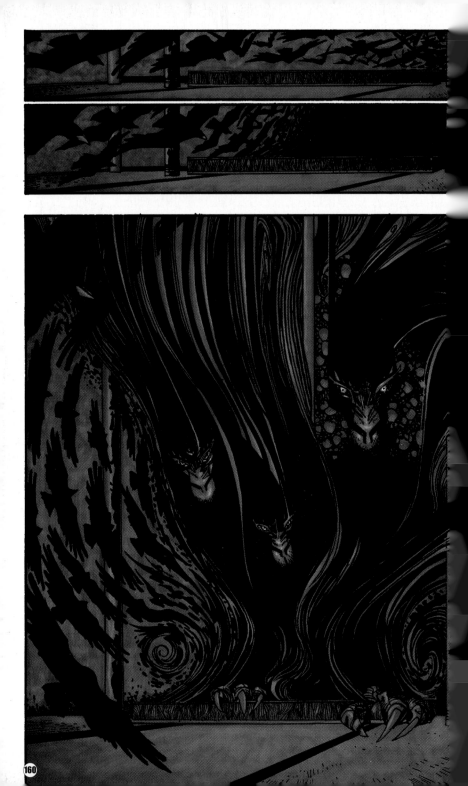

GENERAL GUO...

...THE WAY I CLEAR

...BUT I FRANKLY DON'T *CARE* WHETHER WORD IS SPREAD OR NOT. LET THEM KNOW THE SONS OF SHINACEA HAVE RETURNED.

WITH WHAT'S LEFT OF ITS ARMY DRAWN TO THE NORTH, NAYADO WON'T BE ABLE TO PROTECT ITSELF EVEN *IF* OUR PRESENCE IS KNOWN.

THIS TIME WE WON'T BE DRIVEN BACK.

WE DON'T EXPECT MUCH RESISTANCE FROM THE VILLAGE. IT'S MOSTLY WOMEN AND OLD MEN.

WE'RE ROUNDING THEM UP TO MAKE CERTAIN NO ONE ESCAPES AND SPREADS NEWS OF THE INVASION.

GOOD...

THIS MISERABLE SCRAP OF AN ISLAND WILL BELONG TO THE AUGUST EMPIRE WITHIN THE WEEK.

I WANT THIS WRAPPED UP AS QUICKLY AS POSSIBLE.

UNDERSTOOD?

YES, SIR.

WE MARCH ON YAZAKI IMMEDIATELY...

"...AND WHEN WE GET THERE I'LL HAVE MITSUMUNE'S *HEAD* AS MY TROPHY."

MEEGH!

ONE OF THE *MONKS!*

YOU KNOW RYUICHI BETTER THAN I, OBO-SAN.

HOW LONG WILL HE WAIT BEFORE THROWING HIS MEN AT THE MONASTERY WALLS?

HE HAS ALWAYS BEEN PATIENT, WULF...

APPARENTLY RYUICHI IS NOT SO *PATIENT* AS YOU BELIEVE.

HE MUST HAVE SENT A FORCE TO ATTACK IN SECRET.

...BUT HE WILL BE LOATH TO KEEP THE ARMY SO FAR FROM THE CAPITAL FOR ANY LENGTH OF TIME.

WE HAVE A DAY, PERHAPS *TWO,* BUT NO LONGER, BEFORE HE CAN FELL ENOUGH TREES TO MAKE LAUNCHES AND—

GODS...

NOT GODS...

GYAAH!

...DEMONS.

..WE'LL SEE HOW THEY LIKE THE TASTE OF STEEL.

ghlid

THEY MELTED FROM THE SHADOWS...

...AND BEGAN *SLAUGHTERING* THE MONKS.

PERHAPS THEY *ARE* THE SHADOWS.

IS IT RYUICHI? DID *HE* SEND THEM?

THIS IS *BEYOND* HIM, AIKO.

WHEREVER THEY CAME FROM...

...WITH SUCH A *TINY* THING?

WHUH?

YOU WOULD CARVE THE SHADOWS THEMSELVES...

WULF!

OBO-SAN...

SOJIROU-SAN?

THEY ARE HERE FOR *YOU.*

THEY DESTROY OUR FELLOW MONKS *SEARCHING* FOR YOU.

"...BUT THEIR OBJECTIVE IS THE SAME AS HIS..."

...*THE WEAPON.*

IT IS YOUR ONLY HOPE.

IT IS YOUR *SALVATION.*

NO. THE WEAPON OF HEAVEN IS *TAINTED* BY THE GODS. I HAVE SWORN TO UNLEASH ITS MIGHT ONLY AGAINST *THEM.*

THAT IS A VOW I WILL NOT BREAK.

FOR ME?

THESE DEMONS ARE SENT BY MITSUMUNE, THEN?

MITSUMUNE IS A SEPARATE MATTER.

THE DEMONS WERE SENT BY ANOTHER...

IS *THAT* HOW HE HAS BEEN RESURRECTED?

AND ONCE YOU VOWED *LOYALTY* TO THOSE SAME BEINGS.

YOU HAVE BEEN GIVEN A *GIFT*, OBO-SAN...

...YOU WILL HAVE NO CHOICE BUT TO *USE* IT.

NO...

173

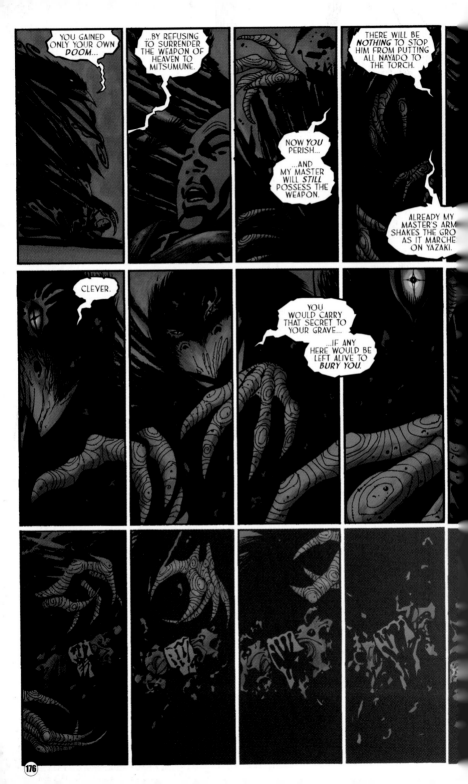

OBO-SAN, ARE YOU *HURT?*

I USED IT...

WHAT?

I *USED* IT. I USED THE WEAPON.

WHAT... HAPPENED?

IT *DESTROYED* THEM.

THAT ONE REELS FROM ITS WOUNDS...

...BUT IT *LIVES.*

AND IT THINKS TO *ESCAPE!*

THEN WE ARE SAFE HERE FOR A TIME?

NONE OF US ARE SAFE.

realistic muscular figures, I'm creating tension and motion with black shapes.

I've been drawing hyper-muscular stuff for most of my life, but that's never been something I completely enjoyed. Superheroes are fine – the heroic part at least – but when the muscles are the focus, the storytelling suffers. Whereas in THE PATH, visual storytelling is the most important thing.

It's a matter of getting closer to the comics I personally enjoy. I've always liked Frank Miller's work, especially the *Sin City* stuff. What first attracted me to it is that Miller stopped trying to draw pretty. He concentrated instead on the storytelling, which was purer because it wasn't glossed up. At this phase of his career he's getting to the essence of graphic storytelling. Every element Miller puts on the page helps tell his story. There's nothing extra. Nothing wasted.

He seems to groove on taking things down to their bare essentials.

And yet at the same time there's plenty of eye candy in Miller's black and white work. The way he uses rain, for instance. He's constantly warping light and space to create a dramatic effect that's not entirely realistic. It's not the same as super-realistic muscles, but it's eye candy that establishes mood and therefore fits the story.

I'm taking a similar approach in THE PATH. I'm not using light realistically. I'm using black primarily to enhance the design of the page and set the mood of the story. Even in my layouts, I'm less interested in displaying an activity than in building drama. A lot of stuff happens off panel. I'll do panels where the only thing you see of the main character is his cheek. All to enhance the dramatic tension.

Bart Sears has been a professional comics artist since 1985. Since then he's worked for just about every major company penciling just about every marquee character. Bart started teaching at the Joe Kubert School in 1990 and wrote a 'How To' column for *Wizard* magazine for three years. He also drew a lot of the early Wizard covers and helped establish that magazine's look.

In the late 1990s Bart went to work for Hasbro as a toy designer, but he kept a hand in comics on titles like Marvel's *Blade* and *Spider-Woman*. Bart arrived at CrossGen in time to launch THE FIRST before moving on to start THE PATH. Bart has since become CrossGen's Art Director.

Whereas his work on THE FIRST is bright and bursting with energy, THE PATH is dark, almost gloomy, and rarely do the figures seem fully defined. Yet for all that THE PATH has a vibrant, kinetic quality that stands out from the rest of Bart's work.

How would you characterize your approach to THE PATH? It looks so different from your past work.

Yeah, it is a big departure. Instead of focusing on ultra-

Miller was one of the first American artists to study Japanese cartooning and try to incorporate some of their approaches in his own work. Are you a manga fan?

Not really. I do read *Lone Wolf & Cub*, which I've always enjoyed. It contains some of the best references for everyday things within that time period. But *Lone Wolf & Cub* is just about the only manga I've read.

Alex Toth has really influenced my approach to THE PATH. Toth is another master of blacks. He's a guy who doesn't go for the eye candy. His simplicity of line and layouts are just beautiful. And he's a fantastic visual storyteller.

To my mind, when you're reading a comic, if you ever have to stop reading the story to stare at the beautiful rendering an artist has put there, then the artist has failed. He's pulled you out of the story. We've all done it countless times. That's the fine line we cross daily when we make comics. And that's one thing I'm trying to get away from in THE PATH.

Are you saying an artist shouldn't put beauty on the page? That there's no room for detail in comics?

I'm saying that the best graphic stories you read without necessarily noticing the art – and that's when the art is most successful.

If you're watching TV and somebody's talking to you, that distraction to me is the same type of distraction as when you've stopped reading to look at the beautiful art. If the art is so exquisitely rendered that it takes you out of the story being told, then the artist has failed.

We've all sat in the movie theater watching a film so bad we started noticing the special effects. But some movies do the opposite. The story is so good and the storytelling so seamless that you only notice the great special effects in hindsight. That's what I'm aiming for in THE PATH.

How do you achieve this spareness, when your work has always been known for hyper-realistic detail?

The essence of my art has always been structure – the basic form over which you construct the figure. Generally, you start with a basic form and keep adding layers of muscle, rendering, costume detail, all that stuff. With every layer of detail, you run the risk of overwhelming the basic form, removing its essential weight and motion.

What I'm doing with THE PATH is putting down a basic form, then choosing the simplest, quickest, thickest black shapes I can put on that form to define the figure. With your first look, you get it immediately. You shouldn't have to figure out the details of a guy's costume to know who he is or what he's doing. And there should be some weight behind the figure. His structure should be sound.

The tool I use most when I'm penciling this book is a thick black marker. Come to think of it, I don't really use a pencil on THE PATH at this point. I do a small half-size page layout, and then I just start with the markers. I do everything with the markers and black shapes, which keeps me concentrated on structure.

If you're drawing in ink, how does your inker earn his pay?

Right now we're scanning my half-size pages, which are very rough – I mean they're not meant to be finished pages. We scan them in, enlarge them 200%, print them out as bluelines, and Mark (Pennington) inks that.

Mark is truly inking on THE PATH. In fact, you could call him a 'finisher.' Mark needs to interpret every single line. There's no tracing at all on that board.

Penciling has become such an anal-retentive medium, where pencilers put down every single line to be inked. Then the inker is supposed to trace those pages. I think that's bull. At least, that's the opposite of how I want to work here.

Earlier you mentioned that your spare approach made it easier to capture motion in your figures. Can you expand on that?

The sparer your penciling is, the less rendered, the easier it is to convey action. A simple line and heavy blacks enhance the motion you can convey in a drawing. I think it falls back to the speed with which your eye sees the image.

I've always felt constrained by a pencil. It comes to a point, and it's made for drawing fine lines. I've drawn a few books in the past where I've used blunt pencils, with soft lead, to try to get more energy and power in a simpler line. I've found with THE PATH that the fat markers are even better for that. If I had to render it in pencil, I'm sure I would noodle it up and add a lot of extraneous rendering and detail. But with the markers there are no do-overs, and that cuts out extraneous detail.

Plus, when I'm penciling with markers and I screw up, I just draw a new panel and paste that over. I try to put the blacks in as quick as I can, because, if I don't, I may overthink it, and that'll make the panel stiff.

For the first four or five issues of THE PATH, I actually enlarged my half-page marker breakdowns, then traced over them with pencil, and that's what I sent to Mark. But Mark convinced me that I was losing a lot of the energy and life of the marker drawings, so we tried blowing up the marker drawings for him to ink, and that's worked just fine.

With THE PATH, you've definitely chosen the double-page spread as your main storytelling unit and the horizontal panel as your design conceit. Why?

Part of it was to keep my interest level up. I've been doing this a long time, and I'm bored with single-page layouts. So the two-page spread is a huge challenge. In THE PATH, it allows for a kind of widescreen storytelling. I can do long thin horizontal panels that have tremendous scope and huge vistas. It also lets me break some hard and fast storytelling rules, which is fun. For instance, in the middle of the page, I may have a series of panels that you can read top to bottom, but don't break up your natural left-to-right reading flow.

The aim of this spread is to show the chaos and quickness of battle without being graphic. You don't really ever see anything. You see guys moving. You see flashes of black. You see a sword. You see feet. But you never see a sword going through a man's body and his guts gushing out onto the floor.

Remember that episode of *Seinfeld*, where George kind of goes against everything he usually does? He just does the opposite. And that makes him successful – he gets the women, and the job, and everything. That's sort of how I approach THE PATH.

For instance, on this spread my first instinct was to have the largest panel or the major focus of the spread be the fight. Instead, I chose to make the largest panel the aftermath of the fight, when Todosi sheathes his sword. And the fight I broke up and conveyed with smaller, thinner panels, which create more chaos and energy. You want to see more, but you can't, and that gives the sequence a kind of nervous charge. It makes you antsy, because you can't really tell what's happening. I like to think it makes for a truer depiction of battle.

And what is happening in this middle tier of panels?

It's quick cuts. In a two-page spread, you can have a large panel on the left side and a large panel on the right, and then between them you can have several horizontal panels in the same tier without confusing the reading flow of a page. That center tier can even have different pacing from those surrounding it. In fact, that's why I use it. For the artist, this approach allows you to direct the readers eye exactly the way you want without anything extraneous.

The overall effect is like a Sergio Leone film – the sudden, jumbled violence, all the reaction shots, the isolated details.

Exactly. The last panel is an example of something I've done a lot in THE PATH, where I'm changing panel sizes to focus on small extraneous actions that aren't necessarily part of the main scene, but could be occurring simultaneously elsewhere. In this case, these guys have sat and done nothing, but they're in the same room. Yet, by changing the panel size, you're pulling out of the one action and refocusing on something else.

In the spread above, the large panel that establishes the setting of the whole scene is depicted in the middle of the page – Obo-san preparing Todosi's body for burial. You see that there are guards around. Wulf and Aiko are waiting patiently. They're having a conversation about Obo-san and what's going on. At the same time Obo-san is preparing his brother's body. So in smaller inset panels I showed the calm, quiet preparations. In the larger panels, where the conversation's going on, you have a different pace. I kept all the conversation panels the same size, and the same placement of the two panel types has a calming feeling. There are no panel size changes. It's all kind of harmonious.

Is there a significance to the symmetry of the page? Do you vary according to mood?

Right, because I'm going for a different mood. The symmetry of this spread and the flat nature of the layout has an underlying calming effect. There's nothing jarring about any of the placements of the figures. There's nothing the reader has to work at. It's all pretty simple and straightforward.

Compare that to the other spread. There's a lot of changes in panel size. It's asymmetrical. Everything's tight within the panels, which leads you to feel there's more going on and you're missing stuff. Until the penultimate panel with Todosi, which is simple and bold and utterly calm.

The job of the graphic storyteller is to control not just the pacing but the time, the actual amount of time covered by the story. That's in the page layout as opposed to the panels. So designing the page is the first step in controlling time, the mood, and the overall energy level.

It seems like there's a lot of contraction and expansion of time throughout the book.

Yes. Very consciously. At least that's my goal. It all serves the story.

Symmetrical doesn't always mean sedate. Here's a page that is relatively symmetrical, but with an extremely violent action. One of the reasons I chose a symmetrical layout for the suicide scene is that I wanted to portray the naturalness of this act for these people. It wasn't an unnatural act, but part of their society. It was violent, but there's a calmness.

I focus on the swords in the first couple of panels rather than faces. Even though they're preparing for this bloody act, the establishing shot in the upper right gets across its ritual nature.

CROSSGEN COMICS®
GRAPHIC NOVELS